# DOCTOR WHO

## The Way through the Woods

# The DOCTOR WHO series from BBC Books

*Available now:*

Apollo 23 *by Justin Richards*

Night of the Humans *by David Llewellyn*

The Forgotten Army *by Brian Minchin*

Nuclear Time *by Oli Smith*

The King's Dragon *by Una McCormack*

The Glamour Chase *by Gary Russell*

Dead of Winter *by James Goss*

The Way through the Woods *by Una McCormack*

Hunter's Moon *by Paul Finch*

*Coming soon:*

Touched by an Angel *by Jonathan Morris*

Paradox Lost *by George Mann*

Borrowed Time *by Naomi Alderman*

# DOCTOR WHO

## The Way through the Woods

### UNA McCORMACK

5 7 9 10 8 6 4

BBC Books, an imprint of Ebury Publishing
20 Vauxhall Bridge Road,
London SW1V 2SA

BBC Books is part of the Penguin Random House group of companies
whose addresses can be found at global.penguinrandomhouse.com

Penguin
Random House
UK

*Doctor Who* is a BBC Wales production for BBC One.
Executive producers: Steven Moffat, Piers Wenger and Beth Willis

First published by BBC Books in 2011
This paperback edition published by BBC Books in 2018

www.penguin.co.uk

A CIP catalogue record for this book is available from the British Library

ISBN 9781785943560

Commissioning editor: Albert DePetrillo
Editorial manager: Nicholas Payne
Series consultant: Justin Richards
Project editor: Steve Tribe
Production: Rebecca Jones

Printed and bound in Great Britain by Clays Ltd, Elcograf S.p.A.

Penguin Random House is committed to a sustainable future for
our business, our readers and our planet. This book is made from
Forest Stewardship Council® certified paper.

MIX
Paper from
responsible sources
FSC
www.fsc.org    FSC® C018179

*For Kat,*
*who also likes Amy*

Between the housing estate and the motorway lies an ancient wood. Birds live there, and foxes, and the many small beasts that snuffle round the undergrowth busy on their own quiet errands. The woods teem with life: sharp, clever robins and blackbirds with bright and restless eyes; owls that sleep by day and quest by night; vivid darting butterflies; and all the wild and thrilling creatures – badgers, and hares, and maybe even a glimpse of a soft-eyed, soft-footed deer with her small fawn. Yes, the woods are filled with life.

But not with people. People – human people – don't go near the woods. The birds are left to nest in peace, the foxes to trot and hunt, the many small beasts to run and hide. And if, on a clear bright day, you took to the skies and you flew high, high above the land, you would see the trees gathered thickly in their hollow, old and dark and patient. You would see how the housing estate backs away from the forest, and you would see too how the motorway strains and bends to avoid it. Screwing up your eyes, you would look for a path leading into the woods – but you would not find one. Because there is no way through the woods. There has never been a way through the woods.

# Chapter
# 1

*England, autumn, just before the ten o'clock news*

Vicky Caine's watch was a sixteenth birthday present from her dad. Vicky Caine's dad was short of cash that month, and the watch was of doubtful origin. But Vicky didn't mind. She appreciated the thought, and she'd almost saved up enough from babysitting to get a proper watch, if she really wanted one. Besides, after sixteen years, Vicky had a pretty good idea of what her dad was like. Fun, but not what you would call reliable.

Unfortunately for Vicky, her dad's gift wasn't very reliable either. Vicky Caine's watch had stopped twenty-two minutes earlier, but Vicky didn't know that yet.

She was babysitting that evening for her parents' friends Carole and Frank, who were at their dancing class. (Carole had made Frank take up tango because of Vincent on *Strictly Come Dancing*.) Vicky took their little boy Alfie up to bed at seven o'clock, read him his Charlie and Lola book (twice), and then she settled down in front of the television. Vicky liked BBC Four, but her older brother, Mark, laughed at her whenever she switched it on at home. Now she had four straight hours, curled up in Carole's brown leather sofa, undisturbed by brothers or fathers. Bliss. Partway through a documentary about the Ancient Greeks, Carole and Frank came back in, cheerful from the exercise. They all had a cup of tea and a chat, and then Vicky noticed the time on her watch. Five to ten.

'Hey,' she said, 'I'm going to miss my bus! I'd better run!'

She grabbed her coat, and gave Carole a quick kiss, waving away Frank's offer of a lift, as she did every week. No point in that when the bus took Vicky almost to her front door. Frank watched her to the end of the street. The stop was no more than minute's walk from there.

It was a chilly night, late in October. During the day there was still bright sunlight and blue skies, but by this time there was a sharp edge to the air, as if the evening had suddenly drawn in its breath. Vicky stood beneath the dull orange street lamp, stamped her feet, and hummed contentedly to herself. After a few minutes, she started to get impatient. 'Come on bus,' she shivered. The last bus was often a bit late. Especially when it was cold.

Another few minutes, and she started to feel uneasy. She pushed up her glove to check the time.

Five to ten.

'Oh, you're *kidding* me...' Vicky tapped the face of the watch. The hands remained locked in place, frozen at an earlier time. 'Oh, *Dad*...'

Who knew what time it was now? Had the bus come or gone? After a couple more minutes of indecision, Vicky heard, very faintly, blown towards her on the slight breeze, the town hall clock. It was chiming the quarter-hour.

That cleared it up, then. She'd missed her bus by a good ten minutes. So what now? She debated popping back and taking up that offer of a lift, but knocking at the door would almost certainly wake up Alfie, and she really didn't want to drag Frank out. Taxi? Vicky sighed as she took out her phone. Taxis were *so* expensive.

No signal. She really was short of luck

tonight. There was nothing else for it...

'Mum'll kill me if she ever finds out,' Vicky murmured, as she set off down the lane. Still, now she had a twenty-minute walk to think up a good cover story. What time did that Ancient Greek thing end? She could say she stayed to watch it to the finish, and then suggest that she'd got a lift... Not outright lie, just *hint*... OK, so Mark would never shut up about it, but even that was better than admitting she'd walked home...

A walk which, so it turned out, was going to take longer than Vicky expected. Barely had she left the bus stop, when the lane started bending in the wrong direction, back towards the houses and away from the junction with Mill Road, where Vicky lived. She tried to picture the route the lane took, but couldn't fix on anything substantial. She had a hazy sense that at some point it had to meet up with Mill Road. Why would a road wander like this? Weren't roads meant to be straight, if at all possible?

'Must be a contour line,' Vicky mumbled to no one in particular. On the bus she had never noticed; she must always have been reading or listening to music. But it was going to add absolutely *ages* to her walk. 'I am in *so* much trouble,' Vicky told the cold clear sky. Some stars twinkled back, sympathetically, but didn't deign to offer any advice. She tried her phone every so often, but still couldn't get a signal. Must be some kind of dead spot, around the edge of the estate.

At last, the houses came to an end. Ahead, the lane curved on, lit at intervals by orange lamps that still bent gently away from where Vicky wanted to be. She stopped to get the lie of the land. In the distance, far behind and to her left, she could hear the soft throb of traffic on the motorway; the sound of safety, of civilisation. The new estate was behind her too, over on the right. Looking back over her shoulder at it, Vicky saw bright squares of light in upstairs windows where the curtains had not yet been drawn: people going to bed on an ordinary Tuesday night, everyday signs of everyday life. Carole and Frank would probably be in bed now, their house in darkness. No, Vicky didn't want to disturb them.

The town hall clock chimed half past ten. Vicky looked ahead. On either side of her lay open ground, fields, cloaked in darkness, although looking straight across the left-hand side she could see what she thought were the street lights at the junction where the lane eventually met Mill Road. Why couldn't a lane simply go *straight* when you most needed it? She crossed the road and stopped at the fence, looking at the beacon of light at the junction. If she cut across the field, she would get straight there. But cutting across the field would bring her very close...

To Swallow Woods.

Vicky shivered again. The woods were creepy. Everyone knew and everyone kept away. Parents didn't have to issue warnings because kids didn't even dare each other to go near. Vicky had never heard a reason, not a particular reason, but everyone knew to keep their distance from Swallow Woods. Probably it was nothing more than children's tales; a memory of a dark and wild place glimpsed when you were small that somehow stuck with you, even when you were old enough to know better.

But the truth was that, right now, Vicky was far more worried about what her mum was going to say when she rolled up well after eleven o'clock. A kid's tale about a scary forest was nowhere near as scary as Vicky's mum when she thought one of her children had done something particularly irresponsible. Vicky rested her hand on the rough wooden fence and stared at the lights twinkling and beckoning over at the junction. If you thought about it, the woods were pretty much the safest place in the area – nobody went anywhere near them. This was the twenty-first century, not the dark ages, and Vicky was sixteen, not six. Who believed there were monsters in the woods?

The decision made, Vicky climbed over the fence and jumped down. She landed with a soft thud on compacted earth, and she was heartened to realise that this was a footpath of sorts. So other people did come this way and, looking at the path, it seemed they did so for the same reason as her: to cut off the loop in the lane and to get as quickly as possible to the junction with the road. So there was no reason to go near the trees. She could steer by the lights, and follow the path. There was no need to go anywhere near the trees. Not that it would matter. It wouldn't matter at all.

The trees sat patiently, a dark and silent mass to her left. Vicky kept her eyes firmly fixed on the street lights. The path quickly became muddier, a mess of tufts of thick grass and clods of wet earth. The ground sloped down to the left, and it proved difficult for Vicky not to be drawn that way. As if the trees were acting like a magnet... but trees couldn't do that, of course.

'You're spooking yourself,' Vicky said. 'You're being stupid.' Her voice came out high and rather thin, but firm enough to be a comfort. She shoved her hands deep into her coat pockets and plodded on.

Then she slipped – on a lump of soil, perhaps, or a tough piece of grass. She fell forwards, tumbling down onto the ground, rolling heavily onto one side. She sat still for a few moments, eyes closed, arms wrapped around her body, making herself take deep breaths until the sick shaky feeling passed and she was sure she wasn't going to burst into tears. She longed to be home, taking her ear-bashing from Mum, bickering with Mark.

Vicky opened her eyes. There was mud all over her coat, her jeans, and her boots. 'I'm in so much trouble...' She stood up, brushing uselessly at herself, only succeeding in smearing mud over more of her clothes. 'Wait till it dries,' she told herself. 'Clean it in the morning. When you're home.' She looked round. Clouds had covered the sky and the stars had slipped quietly away. She could no longer see street lights, in any direction.

For one brief, awful second, Vicky panicked. She heard herself moan, and she clamped her hand over her mouth. 'You have to go *up*,' she whispered into her glove. 'The trees are in the hollow. If you go *up*, you'll find the road.' And as soon as she found the road, she would stick to it. She would never come this way again. She would never come this near to the trees. It wasn't worth it.

She took one tentative step forwards. Then another, then another. She wasn't certain, but it felt like she was going up. But the night was very dark now, and the throb of the motorway very distant, and a hill can rise again before sloping away. The trees were silent and invisible, and long before she realised what she had done, Vicky entered their embrace. A fox, which had been sitting and watching with interest as she stumbled ever nearer to the woods, sniffed at the chill night air, coughed, and then trotted after her. And that was the last anyone saw of Vicky Caine for quite some time.

# Chapter
# 2

*England, autumn 1917, shortly before closing time*

Emily Bostock smiled at the young man sitting by himself at the far side of the pub. He smiled back, as he had done every time. Nice smile, this one, perhaps a bit lop-sided and not so sure of itself, but kind, Emily thought. Yes, he looked very kind.

Annie, the landlady, tapped Emily on the arm. 'There's a table over there that could do with a wipe.' She nodded towards the young man and gave Emily a conspiratorial wink. 'That table too, maybe, on your way back?'

'Maybe,' Emily said, not wanting to commit herself. No need to rush now, was there? Where did that get you?

'He looks nice,' Annie said. 'That's all I'm saying.'

Emily picked up a cloth and gave it a shake. 'Never said he didn't, did I?'

Annie laughed. Emily, smiling, headed off to gather up empty glasses, swapping a few words with the regulars as she went round. She kept half an eye on the nice young man, though, wondering who he was, where he'd come from. She'd never seen him before this evening. He had walked in twenty minutes after they reopened, eaten a huge piece of pie, and sat there in his corner ever since, sipping at one pint of ale. He stuck out like old Frank's red nose, and he'd earned himself a fair amount of muttered comment from Frank and his cronies as a result. Not just because he was a stranger, but because he was young. Only the old men drank at the Fox these days. The young men were all gone away.

'Well,' Emily said briskly, clattering the glasses together, 'there it is.' She glanced again at the young man. Good gracious, he was staring right at her! That was forward! Emily blushed hotly. Frank and his gang of old wasps hadn't missed it either; the story would be round the village in no time. Emily hurried her pile of glasses into the back, where she lingered over the washing up and wondered whatever this young stranger could be about.

When she came out front again, an unpleasant silence was hanging around the bar, like dirty old smog over a city. The young man was still sitting by himself, but now he was staring down at a white feather that had somehow found its way onto the table in front of him. He seemed bewildered, like he couldn't quite believe what he was looking at.

Emily saw red. Hadn't this lot done enough damage by now? Weren't they satisfied? Annie gave her a worried glance and opened her mouth to speak, but before she could get a word out, Emily called across to the young man, making sure her voice carried to every nook and cranny of the pub. 'Don't you pay any attention to this lot,' she said. 'The closest any one of them's been to France is a day trip to Brighton.'

The silence in the room changed, like everyone had stopped hungering for a reaction and instead suddenly became embarrassed or ashamed. So they should be. Blood pumping in her ears, Emily threw her dish cloth over her shoulder and stalked back out. Slowly, she washed her face and hands in the big sink, cooling her cheeks and her head. Funny how she didn't want to cry. This time last year she would have been in floods. Perhaps she was past that now. She wasn't sure whether that was a good or a bad sign. She didn't ever want to forget…

When Emily came out front again, hardly any of the drinkers met her eye, and those who did quickly looked away. So they should. The evening was quiet after that, subdued, and when Annie rang the bell for closing time, Emily made a big show of walking over to the young man. 'If you wait,' she said, loud enough for everyone to hear, 'you can walk me home.'

She heard the stir behind her. She tossed her head.

The young man glanced past her, rather nervously. But he said, 'Great! Yeah! I'll wait. Of course I'll wait!'

Annie didn't make her stay. 'I'll clear up. Don't want to keep him hanging around while you wash up, do you?'

So Emily washed her hands again, straightened her hair, and pinned on her hat, the one with the jet-black butterfly pinned to the crown. It wasn't her best hat, but it was definitely an eye-catcher. A proven success. The young man stood by the door and smiled at her as he waited.

'What's your name, then?' she said.

'Rory.' He was twiddling with the white feather between his fingers. They were long, expressive fingers that looked like they might do much of his talking for him.

'Just Rory? Nothing else? Or do you come with a whole name of your very own?'

He laughed. 'Williams. Rory Williams.'

She stuck out her hand, feeling very modern. 'And I'm Emily Bostock. Very pleased to make your acquaintance, Mr Williams.'

He shook her hand. 'The pleasure's all mine, Miss Bostock.' Then, sweetly, he took her shawl and placed it around her shoulders. Nice smile, and nice manners too.

'Well,' Emily said. 'Are you going to walk me home or not?'

'I think I should.' He pushed the door open, stood back, and bowed. 'After you, Miss Bostock.'

'Why, thank you, Mr Williams!'

Outside a nearly full moon poured milky light upon the lane. The sky itself was stained indigo dark and there was a faint bite to the air. Emily pulled her shawl tighter around herself and glanced back at her companion. His face was in shadow as he closed the door behind them. Now they were alone together. All of a sudden, Emily felt shy. Not such the modern girl after all, was she? And it was a while since she'd been by herself with a young man.

They stood on the step staring at each other, warm yellow lamplight spilling onto them through the windows of the pub. Yes, he had a nice face this one, not what you'd call striking, not exactly, and with a few worry lines, but, well – *nice*. Suddenly Emily felt quite breathless, like she was doing something she oughtn't, but didn't care. She felt quite free.

'Er,' her companion said, after a moment or two standing like this. He lifted his finger as if wanting to attract her attention, while not actually causing any bother, 'I don't know, you know, where you live…'

'Oh, of course, silly me!' Emily pointed past the grey silhouette of the old mill towards Long Lane, winding its way across the darkened fields. 'Out that way. Not quite four miles.' She bit her lip. 'Not too far for you, is it?'

'No, not at all.' He offered her his arm; she linked her own through it, and they walked companionably down the road and turned onto Long Lane. Williams had turned shy; he would catch her eye, open his mouth to start up a conversation and then close his mouth again and smile at her instead. With his free hand, he was still fiddling with the white feather. Maybe that was what was making him bashful.

'I hope you're not too upset about that,' Emily said, nodding towards the feather. 'Nobody with any sense hands them out. Disgusting thing to do, if you ask me.'

'Sorry, what?'

'Your white feather. You weren't too upset by all that business, were you?'

He looked at the feather, as if he hardly remembered he still had it. He gave a nervous laugh. 'Upset? Why would I be upset?'

'Well, you know...' Emily tried to think of a delicate way of putting it, because you couldn't outright say to a young man, particularly such a nice young man, *They think you're a coward because you're not in uniform*. 'They give them to those who haven't been out there... You know. As an insult.'

The penny dropped. 'Oh! Yeah, I see. Probably should have thought of that.'

'Maybe next time keep your silver badge on or something. Well, I'm glad you weren't offended, Mr Williams, but where've you been that you don't know what handing out a white feather means?'

'Here and there.' He waved the feather around vaguely. 'You know how it is.'

'You'd better not turn out to be a spy,' Emily said. 'I'd never live that one down.' She gave him a long sideways look. 'Here, you're not a spy, are you?'

'No,' he said. 'I'm not a spy.'

'Well, I doubt you'd tell me if you was, so I'll just have to take your word for it, won't I?'

''Fraid so!'

'Well, spy or not, you're not to mind.'

'Mind? What am I supposed to be minding?'

'The feather, you daft thing!' Emily slapped his arm, gently – and left her hand resting there. 'No, you're not to mind. What do that lot in there know about the War? Not a thing. Not one thing. None of them are going to get their call-up, are they? All too old. You'd be better sticking Jack Jones's old pig in a uniform and sending that out. Oh, it's easy to be brave sitting with your pals in the Fox all warm and with plenty of beer to hand, isn't it? Not so easy when you're stuck out there in the mud with the fleas and the rats for company.' Emily felt her eyes prickling. She was probably saying too much, but she didn't care. She was past minding her words on account of others. 'Besides, they've got no idea why you're at home, have they? You could have been wounded, couldn't you?'

A sudden, dreadful thought crossed her mind. 'Here, you're not a conchie, are you? Because I'd never live that one down neither.'

'A conchie?' he said. 'What's that?'

She stopped in her tracks. 'A conscientious objector, of course – here, how do you not know that? Where *have* you been?'

'Nowhere, Emily, honestly. I've just... had a lot on my mind recently. But, no – I'm not a conscientious objector.'

'Have you been in the army?'

He hesitated before answering. The moon disappeared behind a cloud and all of a sudden she couldn't make out his features any more, only dark shapes and shadows. 'No,' he said. 'Well, sort of. It's difficult to explain and I can't say any more, Emily... Um. Careless talk costs lives, you know, that kind of thing...'

'You shouldn't say if you don't want to. Don't tell me a lie, though.'

'I'm not a spy, and I'm not a conchie.' The moon came back and again she saw that lop-sided smile, enough to turn a girl soft. 'I don't think I'm a coward either. But you'll have to take my word for that, too.'

'Well,' Emily said gently, 'what sort of world would it be if you couldn't take a young gentleman at his word?' She patted his arm.

'You're a nice lad, aren't you, Mr Williams? You listen. Most lads soon stop listening or never start in the first place. You can tell a good lad by the way he listens. Not much for a girl to ask, is it?' Reaching out, she took the white feather from him and stuck it into her hat, next to the little jet butterfly. 'There,' she said. 'Because we're all in this together, aren't we?'

'Yes,' he said. 'You're right about that.'

The stars twinkled brightly in the unpolluted sky. Emily looked round at the dark fields. She felt all shy herself, now. They weren't so far from the village and she wondered if anyone could see them. 'Oh, I can't stand how long this bloomin' walk takes. Every bloomin' night. Let's take the shortcut.'

Her companion looked doubtfully across the dark field. 'I can't see a path—'

'There is one,' Emily said, 'if you know your way. Don't worry, Mr Williams, I won't drag you into the woods!' She crossed the lane, clambered onto the fence and hopped down the other side. 'I can give you a hand if you need it,' she said, cheekily.

'I *think* I'll manage…' Carefully he climbed onto the fence, and sat on top, legs straddling it. He looked ever so uncomfortable, like a hen perched on top of an unexpectedly large egg.

Emily laughed. 'You have to be a city boy – it's like you've never seen a fence before tonight!'

'Actually, I'm from a village, it's just I'm not usually the one doing the climbing.'

'Got a pal to do it for you?'

'Something like that.' He swung his legs over and jumped down.

'Everyone needs a pal, Mr Williams. I'll be yours if you'll be mine.' She held out her hand, and he took it – and suddenly the laughter bubbled up from inside her like a little brook, the way it used to with her Sam, and Emily broke into a run, pulling her companion after her across the dark field and down into the hollow.

The trees came from nowhere. Mr Williams yanked Emily's arm so hard she came to a sudden halt.

'Ow!' Emily dropped his hand to rub her shoulder. 'Oi! That hurt!'

'Sorry! Sorry! We were getting very close to the trees.'

'The trees? Don't tell me you believe all that nonsense about the woods?'

'The nonsense?'

'Swallow Woods,' she said. 'Haven't you heard – they swallow you up!' She wiggled her fingers spookily. 'Nonsense.'

Williams peered through the branches, as if trying to catch a glimpse of something. 'Don't underestimate old stories,' he said. 'Stories are powerful. And nonsense is sometimes a word for something we don't quite understand, yet.' He looked back towards the lane. 'Perhaps we should keep to the path,' he said, more to himself, it seemed, than to Emily. 'Perhaps we should find out where that takes us. If there's a path, there has to be a *reason* for the path…'

'It's a shortcut. It doesn't go near the woods.' Emily felt put out that he was no longer paying her any attention. All this was spoiling the mood. 'You're not afraid of some bloomin' old trees, are you—?'

'Ssh!' He held his finger up to his lips.

'Don't shush me, Lord Muck!'

'Listen!' he whispered. 'Can you hear it?'

'I can't hear a thing…' He was starting to frighten her. She was painfully aware now that she was alone in a dark field with a complete stranger. But the man didn't make any move to hurt her. He kept on listening for a while, and then shook his head.

'Funny,' he said, to himself again, like she wasn't there. 'If I didn't know better, I'd say it was a motorway…'

'A which-way?'

He turned to her and smiled. 'I'm sorry, Emily,' he said. 'Didn't mean to startle you. I… Oh, don't worry about it. Shall we go back to the path?'

'I don't want to go back to the path,' Emily said. She felt scared now, tricked, as if she had been brought here under false pretences. 'I'm not sure I want to go anywhere with you.'

'OK… Er… Well, we can stand here for a bit… If you'd rather.'

'I'm not sure I want to stand anywhere with you, neither!'

'Then what do you want to do? We'll do whatever you want.' Williams held his hands up, a peace offering. 'I don't want to scare you. I'm not scary, you know. I'm very ordinary.' He looked it too, an ordinary young man completely bewildered as to what he'd done to upset a young lady. Emily suddenly felt very foolish, and very sad. 'What do you want to do, Emily?'

'Oh, I don't know!' Emily cried. Why had she come out here with this young man? What had she been thinking? Everyone had heard her say he could walk her home. She'd be a laughing stock in the morning. But why shouldn't she come here with him? She was twenty years old, and her heart was broken, perhaps beyond repair – and what she wanted most of all was to feel alive again, young again, as young as she'd felt that night two years earlier when Sammy finally plucked up his courage and slipped the ring on her finger. Turning her back on Mr Williams, Emily walked slowly and deliberately towards the trees.

'Emily… Er, what are you doing?'

Emily looked up at the sky. It was cloudy; the moon and the stars were gone. When she looked back over her shoulder, she could no longer see Williams through the dark. Something of her old spirit flared up within her.

'Catch me if you can,' she said and, with a laugh as young as spring water, she ran into Swallow Woods. Behind her, she heard Williams yell, 'Emily! Wait!' An owl, startled by the commotion, flapped up from its branch and hooted out its grievance across the empty silent fields before swooping off, high over the hollow. The two young people passed beneath the trees. Their leaves shuddered, and then turned unnaturally still. And that was the last Amy or the Doctor heard of Rory for quite some time.

# Chapter
# 3

*England, now, four days later*

The clock on the wall was a perfectly ordinary clock, the kind of clock that could be found in any institutional setting on practically every planet. The planet in question being Earth, this clock displayed (in perfectly ordinary circular fashion) a clear set of numbers ranging from 'one' to 'twelve'. It also had an hour hand, a minute hand, and a second hand which ticked resolutely and didn't lose time in such a way as to make life inconvenient for anyone. All told, this was a perfectly ordinary clock.

The wall upon which the clock hung was also ordinary, and the room of which the wall formed one side wasn't particularly distinguished either. It had four stackable office chairs, a decent-sized table on which sat some recording equipment, a door with a lock, and a window with a view onto a car park. There was a blind on the window, but that was broken, and had been for several weeks. People kept forgetting to write the memo. The blind slumped diagonally down across the window, and was likely to remain in this position for some time yet. People had other things on their mind.

About the only thing that wasn't exactly ordinary about the room was the man sitting behind the table. This man was on the youngish side of indeterminately aged, relatively tall, and he had unkempt hair and two pairs of loose limbs that looked as if they would fit more properly onto an entirely different body. The man wore a nice bow tie and an exasperated expression. He had spent the last forty minutes alternating between drumming his fingers on the table top and swinging back on his chair. About four minutes earlier he had started to get seriously bored.

The door swung open and two detectives walked in (for this ordinary room was one of many that, when put together, comprised a decent-sized if ordinary small-town police station). The man in the bow tie looked up.

'Look,' he said, 'is this going to take much longer? Because the fact is I'm actually on quite a tight schedule and if that clock of yours up there is accurate – and I imagine it's accurate, you all seem like very sober and responsible people, and it seems like a very sober and responsible kind of clock – then I need to go and chase down a couple of young women.'

The two detectives – an older red-haired man, and a younger blonde woman – looked at each other.

'I'm afraid that won't be possible, sir,' said the older one, as he took his seat.

The younger detective sat down next to him and reached across to switch on the recording equipment. 'Interview recommenced at,' she glanced up at the clock, 'ten thirty-seven.'

'You seem to spend a lot of time on the road,' said the older detective. 'Do you travel around with many young women?'

'Ah,' said the unordinary young man. 'Now. I see where you're heading with that question, and I want to make it perfectly clear right away that none of them have ever come along unwillingly. Besides, it's strictly invitation only.' He considered these last statements. 'Well, I suppose there was the history teacher. And the air stewardess. But they both had opportunities to leave and they both decided to stay... I'm not helping myself, am I?'

There was a slight and very strained silence.

'I do need to get going, though,' the young man said. 'Things have turned out not to be as perfectly straightforward as I'd anticipated.'

'Have you ever met a young woman called Laura Brown?'

'No. And I haven't met Vicky Caine either... Oh, you hadn't mentioned her yet, had you? I'm really not helping myself, am I?'

'If there is anything at all that you would like to tell us,' said the older detective, 'now is the time to do it.'

'How about – if you want to find your two missing girls, then you should let me go immediately because you are dealing with a situation way beyond your comprehension? No? No, somehow I didn't think you'd be persuaded. Oh dear, this is going to cause us some difficulties... What can I tell you...? Ah! There is something! Something that's been bothering me.'

The young man put his elbow on the table and leaned forwards, beckoning to the two detectives to come closer. His eyes were very dark, shadowed, and they didn't give anything away. Half-unconsciously, half-unwillingly, both detectives leaned in to listen.

'Somebody,' the young man whispered, 'really ought to fix that blind.'

Two hours later, the police press conference about the two missing girls was getting ready to start. The TV journalists and news reporters had been gathering in the town square for the last hour like crows from a Hitchcock movie. The area directly in front of the police station was packed out; some of the cameramen had resorted to standing on the steps leading up to the war memorial in order to get any pictures at all.

Jess Ashcroft made her way through the crowd, ignoring the complaints of those she passed as she pushed doggedly through. Three or four feet from the front, she stopped, peered over the last few heads and nodded, satisfied that she was close enough to see. Just about. She dumped her bag on the ground, rummaged around, and pulled out a pen and notepad.

'Nice moves,' said a voice in her ear.

Jess looked round. The speaker was a bone-thin young man, expensively clad, holding a mobile phone like it was part of him. She recognised him at once from one of the news channels.

'Big story,' said Jess. 'I don't want to miss anything.'

'Quite right!' He grinned at her. White teeth. Cute as a button. 'I like your style, though.'

'You know what the old song says. Dedication's all you need.'

He laughed. 'Good for you! So, what do you make of the whole thing?'

'Well…' Jess didn't want to play all her cards, not all at once. 'Must be awful for the families, mustn't it?'

'Yes, yes,' he said, rather impatiently, 'but the police kept the first one quiet, didn't they? There's something weird going on there.'

'Laura Brown *is* eighteen years old,' Jess said cagily. 'An adult. Well within her rights to get up and go wherever she likes.'

'Nah…' The TV journalist shook his head. 'Doesn't make sense. She was studying for A levels. Fundraising for a trip to Africa. Not the type to disappear into the blue. Yet the police don't seem to have been bothered until the second one went missing. You have to wonder whether it would have helped poor Vicky Caine if she'd known there was kidnapper on the loose. I think someone's head will roll over this.'

Jess chewed her pen. In fact, it had been

no surprise to her that a second girl had gone missing. She'd been dreading the news ever since her younger sister, Lily, had texted two weeks earlier that her school friend Laura Brown wasn't answering calls and her Facebook page hadn't been updated. Jess had been waiting almost unconsciously to hear who was next.

'Exam pressure?' she said, not believing that for a second. 'It can hit some people hard.'

'Not likely to hit both of them, though, is it? I'm Charlie, by the way.'

'I know. I've seen you on the telly. I'm Jess, from *The Herald*.'

His expression changed from friendly interest to friendly pity. 'Local paper? Bless.'

'It's not *all* cinema listings and fake horoscopes, you know.'

'No, I bet it's not. I bet your octogenarian birthday coverage is first rate.'

'Say what you like, but if anyone's going to get a break on this story, it'll be someone with local knowledge.'

'Someone like you, you mean?'

'Well, why not?'

Charlie laughed. 'Then I'd better stick close to you, Lois Lane.'

'Oh yes, very funny, chuckle chuckle. My kid sister likes that one.'

'Keep your hair on, Lois. We're all in this together.'

'I think it helps to know the town, that's all.'

'Ah, and you're probably right. Hey,' he nudged her, 'eyes forward. Here comes Inspector Knacker of the Yard. Not that he'll have anything new to tell us.'

'You think so?'

'What's he told us so far, Lois? It's his head for the chop, I think. Bet you five quid he won't tell us anything.'

'Fine by me. Because I bet he's going to tell us they've made an arrest.'

'Fighting talk! What gives you that idea?'

Jess tapped her biro against her nose and then pointed the tip of the pen towards the policeman. 'Shush. I want to listen.'

Detective Inspector Galloway waited patiently on the steps while the cameras flashed and a yell of questions leapt up, like the barking of hounds. Jess liked Galloway; she'd interviewed him a couple of times in the eighteen months since his arrival in town from Inverness. She had found him preternaturally polite and unfailingly helpful. Poor man. He looked dog tired, as if he'd been dragged through a ditch and then forced into a suit. The suit looked like it had been having an even worse time.

'I'll be making only a short statement right now,' Galloway said. 'I cannot of course comment on an ongoing investigation.'

'Inspector,' someone called from the crowd, 'there've been some questions as to why the police were so slow in investigating the disappearance of Laura Brown and whether this contributed at all to the disappearance of Vicky Caine. Can you comment on that?'

'I cannot comment,' Galloway said patiently, 'on an ongoing investigation. I shall be reading out a short statement—'

'Inspector,' someone else shouted, 'can you confirm that no searches have as yet been carried out in the woodland area north of the motorway? Can you say why this is the case?'

Galloway hesitated. Jess, watching him, sucked in her breath, sharply. Was he about to go off script? What on *earth* would he say?

But Galloway collected himself. He cleared his throat and started again. 'I'll just read out a short statement,' he said. 'I can confirm that an arrest has been made in connection...' All around the square, cameras began to flash, throwing Galloway briefly off his stride. '... an arrest has been made in connection with the disappearances of Laura Brown and Vicky

Caine. A white male, mid-twenties...' Galloway stopped and blinked into the cameras. 'A white male in his mid-twenties is currently helping us with our enquiries. That's all I can say at the moment.'

The clamour of questions rose up again immediately – '*Inspector, can you confirm that this is now a murder enquiry?* – but Galloway turned and went back into the station.

Jess breathed out. She felt a deep sense of relief, as if some kind of disaster had been narrowly averted. She took off her glasses to rub her eyes.

Beside her, Charlie was opening up his wallet. 'I'm impressed,' he said, handing over a fiver. 'Honestly. And I take back what I said about you being Lois Lane. You're obviously Sherlock Holmes.'

'Hmm.' Jess wiped her specs clean and perched them on her nose again. She peered school-marmishly through them at Charlie. 'Sherlock Holmes was a detective, you know, not a journalist.'

'Lois it is, then.'

'Or you could call me by my name. Which is Jess.'

'Come to the pub, Lois. A gang of us are heading over later to the one on the corner. The

Fantastic Fox—'

'That will be the Fancy Fox.'

'Hey, you really do know everything! Whatever it's called, we'll be there from around seven. Come and meet some people. Get your name about. I promise I won't tell them it's Lois.' He went on his way with a wave. 'See you later!'

Jess bent down to pick up her bag. When she stood up straight again, she found herself staring directly at a stripy scarf. The wearer of the scarf was a young woman clutching a supermarket plastic bag in front of her so tightly that her knuckles had gone white.

'It's Jess, isn't it?' she said. 'You're Jess Ashcroft.'

'I am she, there is no other.'

'Oh, at *last*!' The young woman practically stamped her foot. 'Where have you been hiding? I've been looking for you everywhere! It's not *that* big a town!'

Unobtrusively, Jess manoeuvred her bag between herself and the other woman. 'Wherever I've been, I'm here now.' She glanced around. The crowd was thinning out, but there were still plenty of people around she could call on for help. If all else failed, her bag was heavy, full of junk, and could probably pack a significant punch if swung. 'Is there something I can do to help you, Ms…?'

'My name's Amy. Amy Pond. No, you can't help me – it's you that needs my help.'

'I do?'

'Yes, you really do. You're next, Jess. You're going to disappear next. But don't worry! This time it should all work out OK. This time, I'm coming with you.'

# Chapter
# 4

*England, autumn 1917, earlier that afternoon*

The TARDIS landed with a groan, like an ancient relative settling down into an armchair after a lengthy lunch. A robin perched on the signpost that pointed down Long Lane towards the mill, tipped its head and studied the blue box with bright inquisitive eyes. The door creaked open. The robin, put out rather than startled, flew away.

Rory Williams – known universally these days as Mr Amy Pond – stepped out of the TARDIS, blinking like an owl in the bright chilly daylight. Nobody else followed him out. Should anyone have been watching – bird, beast, human, other – they would have seen him turn round, as if suddenly in doubt, only to find the way back into the TARDIS entirely and quite mercilessly barred by his new wife and her pet time traveller.

'Look,' Rory said, in the slightly desperate tone someone might use when he knows that a critical moment has arrived but holds out no particular hope that his very real and pressing concerns are going to be heard. 'It's all very well dumping me here in the middle of nowhere, but the last time that happened I ended up waiting thousands of years. Not an exaggeration! Actually thousands! And I was plastic. Plastic! Do you have any idea what it's like, being plastic? Actually plastic!'

'Actually,' said the Doctor, 'that wasn't you.'

'It could have been me! It might still could have been me! Frankly, it's not hard to imagine it being me!'

Amy ruffled his hair. 'Poor Rory,' she said, with perhaps more glee than sympathy. 'You're your very own action figure.'

The Doctor at least had the courtesy to try a more conciliatory line. 'I promise you'll hardly know we're gone. An afternoon's work, that's all. Well, an afternoon and a bit. An afternoon and an evening. Possibly some of tonight as well… What I mean is, it'll all be over by this time tomorrow.' The Doctor thought about that. 'Your time.' He thought some more. 'Ish.'

'Thanks,' said Rory. 'I feel much more confident now.'

'Think of it this way,' Amy said. 'I get to go and visit our own time. Wow. Thrilling. Can't wait. Meanwhile, *you* get to spend a nice afternoon in a country pub. A real historic country pub, while it's actually being historic. So enjoy the moment! Live it up! Feel the vibe! Drink the beer!'

'Eat the pie,' suggested the Doctor. 'It'll be good honest country pie.'

'And there'll be yokels. You can watch them doing… yokel things.'

'Ooh, and you get to chat up a pretty girl,' said the Doctor; seeing Amy's expression, he hastily corrected himself. 'Or not. In fact, I strongly suggest you do absolutely the opposite of that.'

'Yes, yes,' Rory said, 'beer, pie, pub, yokels – it all sounds very nice, and it probably would be, if it wasn't slap bang in the middle of *the war to end all wars*—'

'Oh, that's *miles* away,' the Doctor said breezily.

'That's all very well for you to say!'

'Different country! There's the whole Channel between you.' The Doctor licked the tip of his forefinger and held it aloft, testing the air. 'Nope, no Zeppelins. Not today. Zip. Nada. No show. Absolutely nothing to worry about! Besides, you'll barely know you were here. These short trips are like bread and butter to the TARDIS. Quick turn of a dial, quick pull of a lever; we're in, we're out, we... um, shake it all about... Yes, well, as I say, nothing to worry about.' He waggled his finger and adopted a lecturing voice. 'What you need to be concentrating on is staying close to Emily Bostock. Don't let her out of your sight.' He dropped the playfulness and went on in a much quieter, much more serious tone. 'What you're doing is critical, Rory. You have to stay close to her. If we lose Emily, we're right back where we started. More importantly, she'll be gone – *really* gone. I might not be able to get her back.'

'I understand,' Rory said. 'Stay close to Emily Bostock.'

The Doctor gave him a kindly smile. 'You'll be fine. Honestly. Afternoon's work. In the pub. With pie.'

'Don't get *too* close to Emily Bostock, mind,' Amy said. 'You're a married man now. And I'll *know*.' She blew Rory an extravagant kiss, gave him a cheery wave, and closed the TARDIS door.

Rory stepped back to watch the dematerialisation.

The TARDIS, however, robustly carried on being there. After a moment, the door opened again and the Doctor stepped out. He had something cupped between his hands and a somewhat sheepish expression on his face. He sidled up to Rory.

'One last thing.' He opened his hands to reveal a small triangular device made from some bronze substance that definitely wasn't bronze. He pressed it into Rory's palm. 'You might want to take this.'

The object pulsed and hummed quietly, as if chatting to itself. Gold specks of light sparkled up and down one flat side like tiny Christmas tree lights. The other side was smooth and blank.

Rory said, 'This is the thing that lets you find me again, isn't it?'

'Um.'

'By "um", you mean "Yes, Rory", don't you, Doctor?'

'Ah.'

'And by "ah", you mean "I'm sorrier than I can possibly say, Rory". *Don't* you, Doctor?'

'Rory, everything's fine. Go to the pub. Chat to Emily,' the Doctor glanced quickly back over his shoulder, 'in an entirely platonic fashion. Keep her close, and keep *that*,' he tapped the bronze triangle, 'with you at all times. When you get where you're going, press that button on the edge there – no, the other edge – and we'll be with you in the blink of an eye.' He closed Rory's hand over the device. 'And when you do go into the woods – *concentrate*. There's nothing there that can hurt you, but you might get disorientated. Don't worry about that. The most important thing is that you don't let Emily out of your sight.' Again, the Doctor gave his kindly, ancient smile, the one that you could only feel proud to get, because it meant someone very wise and very special trusted you beyond measure. Rory couldn't help but be pleased to receive that smile.

'We'll be back before you know we're gone,' the Doctor said, which turned out to be completely true, in a manner of speaking. With one last vast grin, the Doctor loped back inside the TARDIS. Soon the old time machine was grumbling and groaning again, and then it was gone.

From his pocket, Rory pulled out a scruffy scrap of paper onto which a map had been scribbled. Emily Bostock worked as a barmaid at a pub called the Fox. The pub stood at a crossroads opposite an old mill. Slowly, Rory's gaze drifted up from the map to the signpost at the corner of the lane. *Brown's Mill*, it told him helpfully. *3½ miles*. Rory burst out laughing.

'Bang on as ever! Thanks, Doctor!'

He shoved the map back into his pocket and set off down the lane. Soon he was whistling, because the day was perfect for walking, the trees green and gold, and the sun not too hot, and there was the promise of a pint at the end. Altogether, this struck Rory as not a bad deal, and almost certainly better than being plastic. Some pleasures stay much the same, whatever the time and place. Trouble, however, comes in many different shapes and sizes.

# Chapter
# 5

*England, now, after the press conference*

Detective Inspector Gordon Galloway had never intended to live amongst the barbarians. Then, on a walking holiday in the Lake District, he fell in love, his eyes meeting the intriguingly green ones of his wife-to-be over a full English breakfast in a pleasant B&B near Lake Coniston. Nearly the first thing Mary said to him was, 'I'm something of a home bird...' And so – after eleven months, a charming courtship, and a delightful wedding – Gordon Galloway applied for, and received, a transfer to his wife's home town.

A town which, after eighteen months of everyday living and slightly over a week into his first major case there, Galloway was concluding was a very strange town indeed.

It wasn't simply that Laura Brown's disappearance had gone unreported for several days. Parents know their children, after all, and technically Laura Brown was an adult. If she had decided to pack up and take an early gap year, that was her decision, and if her parents had assumed that was what she had done, that was theirs. And as soon as it was clear that something else was happening (when Vicky Caine's frantic and Scouse father turned up at the station to report the non-appearance of his daughter), the Brown family had become as accommodating (and as frightened) as Galloway might have expected.

No, he didn't suspect the Browns, not least because of the strength of their alibis. But there was still something strange. Take that moment earlier today, when he had gone to inform both sets of parents that he had made an arrest, and Laura's mother and father – Vicky's mother too – had stared at him as if he had said he was planning to search the dark side of the moon. It was as if the three of them couldn't quite believe what he was saying.

Vicky's father – who wasn't local, after all – had reacted more as Galloway had expected:

*Who is it? Do we know him? How did you catch up with him?* Then the other three had joined in – but it still hung there, that split second, when they had all stared at each other, clearly all thinking the same thing: *How can that be possible?* Yes, much as it pained him even to think it (for Gordon Galloway was very much in love with his wife) there was something very strange about this town.

Then there was the not so inconsiderable matter of the searches. Vicky Caine's last known location was a bus stop on Long Lane. Laura Brown had last been seen leaving the Fancy Fox pub. Between these two points lay a large piece of woodland. Galloway had several times ordered a search, but somehow it didn't seem to happen. People found themselves elsewhere, or something pressing turned up, or the searchlights were broken and had to be replaced. Each delay was perfectly reasonable. But the upshot was that the search of Swallow Woods had not yet got started.

And then there was the chief suspect…

Galloway glanced across his desk to where his junior colleague, DC Ruby Porter, was talking on the phone. Porter was a pensive young woman that even Galloway thought was slightly too sensible for her age. He went and made them both a cup of coffee. By the time he got back, she had finished her call, and they sat sipping hot instant stuff from nearly clean mugs.

'Tell me,' said Galloway, 'do you think we have the right man?'

'Absolutely.'

'Why do you think that?'

'Um. Intuition?'

'Go on, you can do better than that!'

Porter peered at him over the rim of her mug. 'I don't want to sound strange, sir.'

Strange. There was that word again. 'Hm. Don't worry about that. Fire ahead. Then I'll tell you what I think.'

'OK… Well, it's not the hair, and it's not the clothes… I don't know, but when we're in there talking to him, sometimes he looks at me, and it's like…'

'Go on,' Galloway prompted.

'It's like he's the oldest person I've ever met. There's the word games, and the chatter, and the nonsense, but sometimes I catch him looking straight at me, and when I look into his eyes, deep into his eyes, it's like I'm staring all the way back to the beginning of time.'

There was a pause. If Galloway had had an audience to his earlier thoughts, he would now have turned round to them and said: *See! See what I mean? This town is strange!* As it was, he simply swirled some coffee around his mouth and then swallowed.

'That's… very poetic, Porter. See, I was only going to say that it was extremely odd that there's no evidence of him being in town until right before Laura Brown went missing.'

Porter turned an interesting shade of red. 'Sorry, sir. But it's the only way I can think of putting it. He seems harmless, but if I think about it at all, he might well be the strangest person I've ever met.'

And coming from someone brought up in this town, *that*, Galloway thought, was practically a testimonial.

They finished their lousy coffee and went back down to the interview room. Opening the door, Galloway saw that his chief suspect was standing by the wall, staring at the clock. When he heard the door open, the young man pointed up at it.

'Is that accurate?' he said. 'Are you quite sure it's accurate?'

'Of course it is. Why don't you sit down, son?'

The young man sat down, slowly. Then, with a quick movement, he reached out and grabbed

Galloway's wrist. Porter's hand flashed out to stop him, but the young man said, 'Stop. *Wait*.'

And for some reason she did. The three of them sat there, motionless as a tableau, all staring down at Galloway's watch. The second hand ticked on, on, on, and each second seemed to have slowed, to be taking an age. And then at last it reached the hour. The young man, looking up, stared straight at Galloway – who, all of a sudden, could see what Porter meant. It nearly scared the life out of him.

'It's time,' said the strange young man with the madcap hair and the clownish bow tie and the fathomless eyes. 'Amy and Jess. It's time.'

# Chapter
# 6

*England, now, the Fancy Fox pub,*
*shortly before 7 p.m.*

Jess got to the Fox early. She claimed the big table to the right-hand side of the pub, dumping her leather bag on it to mark the territory as taken. She got a gin and tonic, and then sat checking her text messages, hoping she looked busy rather than worriedly waiting for a group of people who might not turn up. One of her messages was from her sister, Lily:

*An ARREST?!!!? Wots this all about, LOIS? Any news on Luara? :-(*

Jess was in the middle of a lengthy reply (Jess made no concessions to the form: her text messages contained full sentences, accurate punctuation, and no missing or misplaced apostrophes – she would also manage to spell 'Laura' correctly), when she realised that someone was sitting at the table.

'I'm really sorry,' she said, adding the last full stop and hitting *send*, 'those seats are taken— Oh. It's you.'

For it was indeed the alarming Amy Pond, clutching her plastic bag as if it bore a designer label. 'Don't run off again,' she said. 'We don't have time, OK?'

'Please leave me alone,' Jess said, in a clear and carrying voice. A couple of the other patrons looked round curiously, decided Jess could handle herself for the moment, and went back to their drinks and conversations.

'Look, OK, all right, I know we got off on the wrong foot—'

'You practically *threatened* me!'

'—but it's really important you hear what I have to say.'

The pub doors swung open. With a gale of laughter, Charlie and his friends entered the Fox. Through clenched teeth, Jess hissed, 'You are about to ruin what could be the most important moment in my career.'

'*This*,' Amy hissed back, 'is the most important moment in your career. Story of your life, Jess.

Happening now, whether you like it or not.'

Charlie, who had ordered at the bar and was looking round, saw Jess. He grinned dashingly and waved.

'I want you to go away now,' Jess said.

'It's about the woods, Jess. Swallow Woods.'

Jess's heart stopped, gulped, then started again. 'The woods?' she whispered. 'What about them? What do you know?'

'I know an awful lot about them – not everything, but a lot. The rest we'll have to find out as we're going along.' Amy stood up. She smiled, rather grimly. 'Oh, you're *so* coming with me.'

Jess glanced across at Charlie, who was now trying to pick up four pint glasses. 'Tomorrow,' she promised. 'Come and see me at *The Herald* tomorrow.'

Jess had never actually seen someone tear at their hair before. Now she had.

'Aren't you *listening*? Tomorrow? It's now or never!'

Charlie arrived with his friends and his tower of drinks, and set the glasses carefully down on the table. The introductions went round. Charlie smiled at Amy, towering and glowering over Jess.

'Hi!' he said. 'Friend of yours, Jess?'

'Not exactly…'

'Oh…' His ears almost twitched. 'A lead?'

*Story of your life*, Amy mouthed at Jess – and Jess knew she couldn't resist. She pushed her specs back up her nose and beamed guilelessly at Charlie. 'Eighty-fourth birthday party,' she lied. 'Twins. Big story for me. Huge. But I'll come back later and tell you your horoscope.'

'We'll be here, Lois. We'll cross your palm with silver and then you can buy the beer.'

'I'll be five minutes,' Jess promised. 'Um. Maybe ten.'

Amy marched Jess over to a table in a quieter corner of the pub, glaring at the man already sitting there until he got up and left.

'You are very strange,' Jess remarked, as Amy started emptying the contents of the plastic bag onto the table. Piles of printouts and photographs.

'I don't have time not to be strange,' Amy said. She sifted through some of the photographs and made a selection. 'Right. Best place to start is probably with the aerial shots – hoo boy, did they ever creep me out! – yes, we'll start with those.' She handed one of the photographs to Jess.

Jess put the photo down on the table and

studied it. As Amy had said, it was an aerial shot of a piece of countryside. A thick dark smudge of woodland took up most of the centre of the picture. Curving around the woods, at the bottom right-hand side of the page, was a strip of grey road. The town took up the left-hand vertical strip of the page. It was very familiar.

'That's Swallow Woods.' Amy jabbed her finger at the dark green patch. 'And *that*,' she ran her finger along the grey road, 'is the motorway.'

'I know,' said Jess, patiently. 'I've lived round here my whole life—'

'So don't tell me you've never noticed.'

'Noticed what?'

'The *road*, Jess! The motorway!'

'What about the motorway? It's a stretch of motorway. It runs from Junction 11 with the bypass down *here*,' Jess pointed to a place on the table just below the bottom left corner of the picture, then swept her finger up and round to a point just above the right corner, 'to Junction 12 *here*. Both junctions get backed up at rush hour. It's a pain in the neck. I write about it every three or four months and nothing changes. Why? Because it's a perfectly ordinary piece of motorway—'

'Did you not see what your hand just did?'

Amy said. 'The *shape* it made?'

'If you've got something to tell me, get on with it. Because right now I could be networking my way into a job in London—'

Amy shook her head. 'You're not going. You won't leave here.'

'Once again, that sounds unpleasantly like a threat—'

'Look at the *road*,' Amy said. She pulled out another picture, another aerial shot of trees and field and road, and then a third picture. Jess shook her head, but she examined them both. There was no new town in these – only the old village, more or less where they were sitting now – and certainly no motorway – although the old road was there, following broadly the same route. But the shape of the woods was unmistakeable. These were aerial shots of the same piece of countryside, over time.

'Look at the roads, Jess,' Amy urged softly. 'They *bend*. They bend around the woods.' She lined the three pictures up alongside each other, and pointed to the one on the far right. 'That's the road the Romans built. They built it on top of the old trackway.'

'Whoa, whoa, whoa – hang on a minute! The *Roman* road?'

Jess grabbed the picture. This road wasn't a

trace, a memory, the bumps and indentations that get left behind and overgrown, the kind of thing that gets Tony Robinson excited on *Time Team*. This was a road – a working road. A road in use. 'This looks like the *actual* Roman road.'

'It is the actual Roman road. You may remember,' Amy said, 'that Roman roads are famous for being straight, unless they've got a very good reason not to be. And you may notice that this one isn't straight. At all.'

She was right too. At the point where the Roman road met what Jess, in her time, would call Long Lane, it took a sharp south-easterly swing. Eventually, where Junction 12 was now, it righted itself, carrying on its steady north-easterly progress. Jess could see how the road could have been straight. But it wasn't straight. It bypassed the woods.

'That isn't the best one,' Amy said. 'Oh no, no sirree! *This*,' she pulled out another picture, 'is the one that really got me going.'

She handed Jess the picture. This time, the road was a narrow brown line. But it followed the same path, and it curved in exactly the same way. It curved to keep away from cutting through the woods.

'Look at the pictures, Jess,' Amy said softly. 'The motorway bends around the woods. So did the old road. So did the Roman road. As long as people have lived here, they've gone out of their way to avoid the woods. That,' she pointed to the thin brown line on the third picture, 'is the trackway. It's Bronze Age. And it bends away from Swallow Woods.'

Jess sat with the Roman photo in one hand, the Bronze Age one in the other, staring between them.

'This picture,' Jess said slowly, holding up the one showing the trackway, 'looks like it was taken yesterday.'

'Sometime last week, actually,' Amy said. 'Or six thousand years ago, depending on how you look at it.'

'Oh, now you're just being ridiculous!'

'Jess.' Amy put her hand upon her arm. 'You've lived here your whole life. You know this town better than most. You know there's something strange about Swallow Woods.'

Jess licked her lips. 'They're just stories. The kind of thing you tell to kids to stop them wandering off by themselves...'

'Yet when I said I wanted to talk about the woods, you came at once. Those guys over there, you could be chatting away to them right now! Fixing up that fancy London job you've always wanted. But you aren't. You're here with me. Because you want to know the secret of Swallow Woods. All your life, Jess. All your life you've been wondering.' Amy started sifting through her papers again. 'You know that people go missing. That the woods swallow them. Not just Laura, not just Vicky – it's been going on much longer than that. If you look into it, just a day's work, you soon find out that people have been disappearing in Swallow Woods for as long as people have been living here. The trackway, Jess. It bends away from the woods. Those Bronze Age people, they knew. Everyone who's lived here, they've known. Because there's a pattern. Every fifty years it happens, give or take a couple of years. Take a look at these.'

She handed Jess a sheaf of papers: old newspaper reports, from the nineteenth century and earlier. Before that was a selection of parish records, the steady rise and fall of births and deaths across the centuries – but when Jess looked closely at the records, she saw that some of the names had no death date, and that each of these had a green mark against them. Whatever the century, the same mark. Different hands, but the same mark; young men and young women, but the same mark. 1917 – two marks. 1861 – three marks. 1814 – one mark.

At the bottom of the pile was the entry in the Domesday Book. There was the parish – St Jude's – and there was the entry for the wood. Someone had carefully cross-hatched through the name. Nobody wanted to own Swallow Woods. Nobody would go near it.

Jess shoved the papers away. 'You've done all this on a computer – I don't know why, but you must have.'

'All right. There's another thing I have to show you,' Amy said. 'I think this will convince you. But you're not going to like it, and I think you should prepare yourself for a shock.' Reaching into the bag, she drew out one last piece of paper.

It was the cover page of a national newspaper. The paper was yellowing and slightly crisp to touch. Jess guessed it was probably a few decades old. She read the headline – *Third Girl Missing* – and then the start of the story beneath. One paragraph had been circled in felt-tip pen: *And with no news on either Laura Brown or Vicky Caine, fears are now mounting for 24-year-old journalist Jess Ashcroft, whose abandoned car was found parked on a country lane…*

'I'm sorry,' Amy said quietly. 'I didn't want to have to show you that. But you have to understand, Jess – I know that you go into

Swallow Woods tonight. I know that you're the next to disappear. There's nothing I can do about that. As far as I'm concerned, you've already gone. But this time – I'm going with you.'

The paper, naturally, was dated tomorrow.

# Chapter
# 7

*England, autumn 1917, well after closing time*

Rory crashed through the trees. 'Emily! Where are you?' He stopped to catch his breath, bending over, his hands splayed out flat on his legs. 'One job,' he mumbled to himself. 'One. Stay close to Emily Bostock. The Doctor's going to kill me. *Amy*'s going to kill me…'

He felt something small and hard bounce off the back of his head. 'Ow!' Again – and then a third time. A muffled laugh came from above. Emily was perched up in the tree, legs dangling down, weighing one last pine cone like a cricket ball. She had taken off her hat, and loosened her long brown hair. It gleamed in the sunshine. She threw the cone at Rory. He fumbled the catch and it fell to the ground.

'All right,' he said. 'You've had your fun! Are you coming down?'

'Why should I come down? It's nice up here.' She patted the branch next to her. 'Why don't you come up instead?'

Why not? At least she wouldn't be able to run away from him again. Rory grabbed an outlying branch and swung himself up beside her.

'See?' she said. 'Isn't it nice?'

'Oh, yes. Lovely.'

'You don't sound like you mean that, Mr Williams. Here, you're not cross with me, are you?'

'No, it is lovely, just… Please, Em- Miss Bostock, I mean. Please don't run off again like that.'

'Gave you a turn, did I?' She patted his hand. 'All right, I won't run off like that again.'

'Thank you, Miss Bostock.'

'Emily will do.'

'Thank you, Emily.'

They sat for a while, each giving the other quick sideways glances, and then looking hurriedly away.

'They're stories, nothing more,' Emily said at last, apologetically. 'I know we're off the beaten track in Foxton, Mr Williams, but even we're in the twentieth century now! Mr Blakeley up at the big house – his son has a motor car! I've seen it!' She swung her legs to and fro. 'It wasn't working, mind. Slid off into a ditch. The steam that was coming up from it!' She laughed. 'Mind you, they're beautiful things. Imagine what it must feel like, speeding along, the wind in your hair…'

'Maybe one day you'll ride in one.'

'Who, me? I shouldn't think so. Nothing exciting happens here. A motor car might be real enough, but nothing happens in Swallow Woods.'

Rory gave her a sad smile. 'But it's already happening. Haven't you noticed?'

'What do you mean?'

'Look around. What can you see?'

'Trees. We're sitting in a tree looking at more trees.'

'Try again,' Rory said. 'Describe exactly what you can see.'

'Well, where there's trees, there's leaves. I can see leaves. Lots of leaves.'

'Go on.'

'There's a little path heading off just in front of us. I think I can hear a stream, up ahead somewhere. And there's the sun, scattered through the breaks between the branches. It's not such a dense old wood as people would have you think—'

'What time did we leave the Fox, Emily?'

'Just after closing time, of course. That's half past nine.'

'Half past nine. And yet there's the sun. When we left the Fox, the moon was out. Remember? It was nearly full. And now...' Rory waved his hand around. 'Sunshine.'

'So? So the sun's coming up. That happens, you know, even in Foxton. Nothing strange about that.'

'But it's autumn. The nights are longer. How long since we left the pub? An hour at most. How can the sun be coming up already?'

Emily drew her shawl around herself more tightly. 'I don't mind saying so, but you're frightening me, Mr Williams.'

'It's OK,' Rory said softly. 'We're not in any danger, not in any real danger. But Emily – please, promise me, don't run off like that again. Because I might not be able to find you, and if you get lost, you could be lost for ever.'

Emily pulled away from him. In a whisper, she said, 'Who are you, exactly?'

Rory Williams thought of himself as possibly the least alarming person of his acquaintance.

Amy – now *she* was alarming. Gorgeous, wonderful, unique – and alarming. And as for the Doctor... Now Rory saw himself through Emily's eyes: a stranger who appeared from nowhere saying bizarre things while the world went suddenly mad... He knew exactly how it felt to be on the receiving end. He reached out to take Emily's hand. It had gone cold, so he started to rub it.

'Who I am doesn't matter, not really,' he said. 'But it's possible that things are going to get weird around here, Emily, weirder than they are already. It's important that you trust me. I'm a friend. I can look after you.'

As he spoke, the sun shone more brightly on Swallow Woods, catching on the dust motes and pollen and dandelion parachutes that were drifting about, making them gleam for the merest second and then disappear. The leaves were gently stirring. It seemed to Rory almost as if they were held in some eternal Maytime – only Emily's hand was still cold.

'All right, Mr Williams,' she said slowly. 'I'll trust you. But you have to tell me what's going on around here. I'm not daft, and you don't have to lie to me, not even to protect me. You shouldn't do that, not if you want me to trust you. Besides,' she said, and gave him a secretive sideways look, 'we all know about the woods. We pretend it's not real, but we all know about it. So what's happening? What's going on?'

'OK. It's difficult, but try this. Ages ago, someone abandoned a machine in the woods. It's been leaking a kind of energy ever since, like the steam from Mr Blakeley's car, and it's made the woods bend out of shape. That's why all these strange things happen – how it can hop from autumn to summer, or day to night.'

'And why the people... well, why they go missing.'

'Yes, that too. It's not magic or enchantment or anything—'

'Well, I know that! Good gracious, this is the twentieth century! I'm not some simple country girl! I was at school all the way up to 13, I'll have you know!'

'Sorry! Yes, of course, twentieth century... Anyway, this machine has been sitting here rotting and the stuff it's made from makes the strange things happen—'

'Like if Mr Blakeley's motor car broke down near a stream, and some metal got into the water so it turned a funny colour and you couldn't drink it without getting sick?'

'That's.... pretty much exactly what I mean.'

'See – not so daft, am I? Is that why you're

here? To fix the machine?'

'Not so much fix it as find it and cart if off for scrap.'

'And then Swallow Woods will go back to being ordinary?'

'That's the idea.'

Emily rested her hand flat against the trunk of the old tree supporting them. 'Poor old Swallow Woods. Everyone scared, and it's not its fault. Seems a shame to take the magic away, even if it wasn't really magic in the first place.' She stroked the crusty bark with her thumb and sighed. 'Suppose it happens to all of us in time.'

She shook herself and, with a quicksilver movement, slid down from the tree. 'And you knew I came through Swallow Woods and you were worried I'd get lost too. That's nice. I thought you were nice, Mr Williams.' She pulled back her hair and set her hat upon her head, shoving a pin in here and there to keep it fixed in place. Then she put the feather and the butterfly straight.

'Can I help?' she said. 'Help you find the machine?'

Rory clambered down the tree. 'Of course. But we have to stay together.'

'So where now?' she said, when he was on

the ground again. 'Where are we heading?'

'What do you think, Emily?'

'Me? What do I know? Don't you have a map or something?'

'How would you map a place like this? Who would come here to map it?'

She shivered, even in the sunshine. 'You're not helping with my nerves, you know. Well,' she pointed at the path, 'I suppose that's as good a way as any.'

So they went that way, and Rory's heart was heavy, because he had not told Emily everything, not quite. Rory knew that Emily Bostock was going to disappear into Swallow Woods tonight. That's what history said: a green mark against her name in the parish records, one of many marks he and Amy and the Doctor had found leading back through time. Rory's job tonight was to follow Emily, not to lead her; to stay close, to find out where she was going and where she had gone – and perhaps, that way, to save her.

*England, 1917, much further from the pub than was intended, early in the afternoon, before the TARDIS left*

Amy watched on the monitor as Rory got his

bearings. Then the TARDIS dematerialised, and she could see nothing beyond the formless, timeless Vortex. 'He will be all right, won't he? Doctor?'

'Hmm?' The Doctor was busy tinkering with another small bronze triangular device, exactly the same as the one he had just given Rory.

'Rory. He'll be all right, won't he?'

'Of course he'll be all right. Rory's a trooper. Trooper Rory. Solid as a rock – and not one of those porous rocks that lets water through. Trooper Rory the non-porous rock, that's what they call him.'

'Those woods, though. They sound creepy. Paths moving and shifting and wandering about...'

'It's not going to be a walk in the park, Amy, no, but it is a perfectly normal side effect of this particular kind of interstellar drive. There can be some disorientation at first, but you soon get used to it. We know from the records that Emily disappears, which means she must find her way to the ship eventually. All Rory has to do is stick with her, and then use *this* –' he threw the device to Amy – 'to signal us so that we can get a fix.'

She twisted the triangular object around between her fingers. 'Looks like a piece of—'

'In *no* way,' said the Doctor firmly, 'does my superbly engineered triangular tracking technology resemble a piece of chocolate. And I certainly wouldn't advise biting into it. It may be good for locating people stuck in spatial warps, but I doubt it's good for your fillings.'

'Fillings? Speak for yourself, mister! I looked after my teeth. Brushed *and* flossed. So this little hoojamaflip is really how we're going to find Rory?'

'When he's found the ship, yes.'

'And the reason we can't land the TARDIS right in the woods is because of the temporal wotsit.'

'On this occasion the wotsit is in fact spatial rather than temporal. Swallow Woods is… well, it's bigger on the inside. And the word you're looking for is warp.'

'Warp,' said Amy. 'OK. I'm with you. Nearly. Run it past me again.'

'Pass me your scarf,' said the Doctor.

'Sorry?'

'Your scarf. That's the woollen thing wrapped around your neck.'

'Oi. Watch it.' Amy undid her scarf and handed it over. It was a good scarf, long and thin and with cheerful bright stripes, and Amy was fond of it. 'You're not going to Doctor it, are you? I want it back. Undoctored.'

'I'm not going to do anything to it. Nothing that I wouldn't do to a scarf of my own. Now, watch and listen.' He pulled the scarf out lengthways and held it in front of him. 'About ten thousand years ago – give or take a few thousand years – somebody landed their exploration ship near Swallow Woods. Crash-landed, I should say. Because the ship broke down.'

'And the AA hadn't been invented yet.'

'That's right. No AA. Not for a while. Terrible time. Unspeakable. Now, the cause of the breakdown was that the ship's propulsion unit malfunctioned.'

'Propulsion unit. Is that Doctor for "engine"?'

'Yes, that's Doctor for engine. A thing that gets you from A to B.'

'I call that a cup of tea.'

Calmly, the Doctor said, 'I can hold on to this scarf indefinitely, you know.'

'All right, all right! I'm listening now. Properly.'

'Good. Now, what you must understand about space, Amy, if you haven't worked this out already, is that it's very big. And if you're serious about getting from A to B, you need something considerably more complex than a nice hot cup of tea. You're not trying to move yourself from the kitchen to the sofa. You're trying to span the vast empty spaces that lie between the lonely distant stars. So how do you do that? In the case of our exploration ship, the propulsion unit – engine – folds pieces of space together.'

'I'm guessing my scarf's about to have its moment of glory.'

'Correct.' The Doctor folded the ends of the scarf together, so that a long loop hung down. 'But you can see how all that space gets pushed somewhere, into a sort of pocket. When the ship broke down, the pilot dumped it in Swallow Woods, where it's been causing havoc ever since.' He tugged the scarf so that the loop swung backwards and forwards. 'This is why people disappear. They're caught in these pockets and can't get back out.'

'So if we took the TARDIS into the woods, it would probably get pulled into one of these pockets too. We'd be as lost as anyone else.'

'Exactly. But what we *can* do is follow a couple of missing people from different times, triangulate back from them to work out the position of the ship, remove the broken propulsion unit, and –' he pulled his hands apart and the scarf went straight – 'escort anyone lost back to their own time. It's a perfectly simple clean-up job. I only wish people wouldn't go around fly-tipping. I'm not a cosmic bin man.'

'Do we know where the ship came from, Doctor?'

'I think so.' Slowly, he began to fold the scarf. 'All a long time ago, though. Sad story. Shouldn't dwell on these things.'

'Keep Buggering On, like Winston said, eh?'

'Always, Pond. Always.'

Amy turned her attention back to the bronze device. 'Tracking people through spatial wotsits. Chocolate definitely can't do that.'

'And then there's the nuts and the nougat. Think of your fillings.'

'I don't *have* any— Oh, shut up! What do you call this locator thingie, anyway?'

'Do you know, I hadn't decided on a name.' He peered at it. 'It's triangular and it triangulates. How about we call it a triangulator? Or is that too obvious? No, let's keep things self-explanatory.' He smiled. 'Would you like your scarf back now, Amy? We've landed, and it's autumn.'

Arm-in-arm, Rory and Emily walked through Swallow Woods. The day – if indeed a single day was happening around them – became warmer and sunnier, as if spring was accelerating towards summer. The birdsong grew louder and more joyous. Rory even thought he could hear the leaves unfurling, a gentle steady rising sound. He didn't feel afraid, more awed at the strange swift transformation taking place around him; at the sense of being very close to living things and yet very far away from anything human. Except Emily, of course. She walked through the woods with her mouth open and her eyes bright, seeming to savour every moment of this rapidly passing spring.

After what might have been an hour (both their watches had long since stopped), the trees moved apart, forming a round glade. Entering, they both gasped and fell silent. It was as if they had walked into a vast cathedral, but one that was living and growing, not made of stone. The trees were huge and thick with dark green foliage; their upper branches were interwoven, joining each tree to its neighbour and thereby forming massive archways through which dark avenues leading out from the clearing could be glimpsed. The air was hushed, as if a service was about to begin in an ancient green temple.

'Emily,' Rory whispered. 'Why are you humming?'

'Humming? Wouldn't dare! Be like whistling in church! There's water over there, though. Must be that you can hear.'

A small pool, deep and still, lay at the heart of the clearing. They knelt side-by-side and drank thirstily. Emily splashed water over her face and hands. When the ripples settled, Rory could see their reflections, slightly distorted, and framed by the tall trees.

'Here, what's that?' Emily said. Rory, investigating where she had pointed, found the remains of a campfire; a few charred sticks and some small bones left over from a lonely sort of supper.

'I wonder who else could be here?' Rory said.

'Could be Harry.'

'Harry?'

'Harry Thompson from Brook's Farm. Haven't seen him in the Fox for nigh on six weeks. Word is he's run off. His call-up was due. Poor lamb, he's a sensitive sort. If the trees have been playing tricks on him, he'll be scared half out of his skin.'

Rory picked up one of the burnt sticks and stirred the ashes. They were cold and dead. 'What would you do,' he said, 'if we found him?'

'What would I do? I'd come back here tomorrow with a loaf of bread and a packet of fags and whatever else he asked for. I wouldn't send anyone out to France, not for all the tea in China. They wouldn't send him now, anyway. He's as good as deserted. They shoot you for that.' She stood up, abruptly, brushing away the leaves and twigs and ashes sticking to her long skirt. In a quiet, fierce voice, she said, 'I hope Harry's here. I hope he's all right. I hope he stays here as long as this terrible, evil war goes on.'

'I hope so too, Emily.'

Rory brushed the cinders from his hands and stood up. Emily was humming again – no, that hadn't been her, had it... Before Rory could explore this thought further, Emily reached over, took hold of his chin, and kissed him firmly.

'Ah!' Rory squawked, when he had possession of his own mouth again. 'Yes! No! I'm married!'

Emily stared at him. Her pupils were wide and dark.

'*Married?*'

Somehow, she made the word sound like an accusation. She raised her hand and slapped Rory hard across the cheek. Then she turned and ran beneath one of the arches formed by the trees.

Rory came to his senses. 'Emily! Wait!' He dashed after her along the path, stumbling in his haste. Was it his imagination, or were the roots of the trees hindering him, slowing him? Soon the path forked. Rory came to a halt and looked desperately first one way, then the other. No sign of Emily – but on the ground lay a single white feather.

'Emily!' Rory cried. He wasn't meant to lose her. He wasn't meant to lose her...

Paralysed by indecision, unsure which way to go, Rory rubbed anxiously at his temples. The trees shifted, and scorching sunlight poured through the gaps between them. Rory's eyes blurred and watered. Again he heard humming – no, not humming, not Emily, and not the water in the pool either, which had been still water and not running... The noise grew louder, more a throb or a thrum, and Rory realised that it was mechanical, as unlike birdsong or the gentle rustle of leaves as it was possible for something to be. Dark patches appeared in his vision. The trees began to spin around him. Everything began to ebb away.

*I wasn't meant to lose her...*

# Chapter
# 8

*England, now, slightly before closing time*

'Don't say anything,' said Amy. 'I'm not quite finished yet.' From the bag, she pulled out one last aerial photograph. She offered it to Jess, who took it with shaking hands.

Only from the grey line of motorway could Jess tell that this was the same area of countryside that she had seen in the other pictures; her part of the world, and generations of her family before her. Any other continuity with the past had been obliterated. All the houses – the 1930s villas, the 1960s estate, the new estate – they were all gone. In their place were empty fields. And where Swallow Woods had been there was a lake.

'Before you ask,' said Amy, 'this was taken fifty years from now. Yes, in the future. And no – I don't know what happens. I *do* know that it happens over the next few days. You're the last to disappear, Jess. Nobody disappears after you, because there isn't a town for them to disappear from, and there isn't a wood for them to disappear into.'

It seemed to Jess that the everyday sounds of the pub – the laughter, the chatter, the chink of glasses, the cheesy tinkle of the quiz machine – were now coming from a great distance. Blood throbbed in her ears.

'These are fakes,' she said. 'It's easy to fake this kind of thing if you know how.'

'Why?' Amy sounded genuinely baffled. 'Why would I do that?'

'Some kind of hoax—'

'Why bother?'

'A grudge, then. Did I go through a red light while you were on a pedestrian crossing? Did I walk past you and not buy a *Big Issue*? Whatever it was, I'm sorry. I didn't mean it, and I'm sorry. But to do something like *this*...' She crumpled up the newspaper cutting. 'It's cruel!'

'I wouldn't do that,' said Amy. 'For one thing, like I keep saying, I really don't have the time right now! Besides, all this I've shown you –

I'm not telling you anything you didn't already know. But you've been denying it. The whole town has been in denial, for centuries. You, your friends, your parents, your grandparents – you've gone out of your way to avoid Swallow Woods. You've only built roads that keep a safe distance. Think of the council meetings, Jess! The planning permission committees! Everyone there, with the same thought in mind, none of them ever saying it out loud – *we mustn't get too close to the woods…*'

Amy picked up some of the papers, flicked through them. 'Back and back, through the centuries, all your ancestors, for as long as they've lived here, they've all thought the very same thing – *we mustn't get too close to the woods.* Why? Why would they think that? *Centuries*, Jess.'

Jess looked unhappily across the pub. Charlie was still there with his friends. They looked happy and untroubled and as if they had a great future ahead of them.

'Yet not all of you could keep away, not entirely,' Amy said softly. 'Every fifty years, something draws people to Swallow Woods. It pulls at you, like a magnet. That's why you stayed here rather than go off to London, isn't it? You knew there was a secret here.

Something huge. Something vast. The story of your life. That's what's kept you here, writing about birthday parties and shop openings and exam results. You were waiting for something to happen, something that would explain everything strange and unspoken about the town. Well, it's happening now. I don't know how it ends. I don't know what turns this place from a thriving little market town to a lake and a ghost town. What I do know is that it starts tonight. It starts when you go into Swallow Woods. You're going, Jess. You can go alone and be lost for ever, or I can come with you and maybe – just *maybe* – you'll come out again.'

The jukebox blared out suddenly, the opening bars of 'You Ain't Seen Nothing Yet'. Jess nearly jumped out of her chair.

'Will you let me come with you?' Amy said. 'Or are you going alone?'

Before Jess could answer, Charlie sauntered over.

'This birthday party is obviously going to be the event of the year,' he said, with a curious look at Amy. 'You two have been plotting all night.'

'Unmissable,' Jess said, as cheerfully as could be managed under the circumstances. 'I'll get you an invitation.'

Charlie laughed. 'Well in case I have to be somewhere less thrilling, here's my number.' He passed her a slip of paper. 'Anyone willing to skip drinks to do a report on an eighty-fourth birthday is either mad enough or dedicated enough to be my kind of person. Twins or not. Give me a call, Lois, if the partying doesn't finish you off first.'

He went on his way with a wave and a smile as bright as city lights.

Jess stared at the mobile number scrawled on the paper. This was her chance, at last. She could go home, have a bath, watch *Newsnight* while Lily complained about it being boring, and tomorrow she could call Charlie and maybe get the interview she had always dreamed of…

A pleasant fantasy, one which Jess knew wasn't going to happen. Instead, she would get halfway home, and then she would turn the car round. She would drive back to Long Lane and park somewhere dark and quiet. Then she would climb the fence and cross the field, and she would walk into Swallow Woods. And then?

'Eighty-fourth birthday party?' said Amy.

Jess stuck the piece of paper in a small pouch at the front of her big leather bag.

'Twins, no less,' she said. 'Our cover story,

you strange and alarming woman. Did you really want the paparazzi hanging round while we go into the woods?'

Amy sagged back in her chair in relief. 'Oh, thank goodness!'

'Story of my life, you said. What exactly am I supposed to do? I must be out of my mind, but I'm coming.'

He woke to a splitting headache and the certain knowledge that he was in trouble. It felt like this was not an uncommon occurrence, even if he was fairly sure that he had never surfaced feeling hung over on an alien spaceship before.

Because that was certainly where he was. Even with his eyes still shut, he could tell – from the throb of distant engines pitched for non-human ears, from the stale thickness of air pushed too many times through recycling. Yes, this was an alien spaceship. Interesting. He seemed to know about spaceships.

Then he opened his eyes, and his world became incoherent once again. Because through his blurry vision, it was quite obvious that he was in woodland; woodland in October, when the leaves were mottled green and yellow, suspended between their summer splendour and their fall, waiting for one mighty gust of wind to rip them from the branches. Yes, this looked like woodland – but it didn't *sound* like it, and it didn't *smell* like it…

Too much contradictory information at once. He clamped his eyes shut.

'Where?' he moaned. 'When? And why oh why oh why?'

Somebody moved alongside him. He cracked open an eye. 'Who? Who's there?'

A young woman swam into view. She had a round pretty face and long brown hair. She took hold of his hand.

'It's me, Mr Williams. Emily Bostock. How are you feeling now? You've been away a while!'

She helped him to sit up. Blinking to clear his vision, he had to agree with his semi-conscious self that they were indeed on board some ship, in what seemed to be a small empty hold of some kind. The walls, when he put his hand against them, were metallic, but patterned like a wood in autumn. They were lit from within, and when his hand touched the surface, the light seemed to gather around it. All very puzzling, but it was not his most pressing worry.

'Mr Williams,' he said. 'Um. Who's that?'

The woman who called herself Emily

sat back on her heels and looked at him in consternation.

'Oh goodness me! Can't you remember your name? You're Rory. Rory Williams.'

'Rory' shook his head. Mistake. Black spots appeared alarmingly in front of his eyes, and for one moment he thought his vision was going the same way as his memories.

'I'll have to take your word for that.' He looked at Emily suspiciously. 'Er, I suppose I can trust you, can't I?'

'*What*? You cheeky, bloomin'—!' The young woman slapped his arm, hard. 'If anyone here shouldn't be trusting anyone else, it's me shouldn't be trusting you! My goodness, I'm not sure you've said a straight word to me since we met!'

'All right, all right!' Rory (he'd go with that) pointed at his forehead. 'Head injury! Possibly fatal! Fatal as in fatal death!'

He couldn't, in fact, remember a single thing he had ever said to this woman, chiefly because he couldn't remember ever having met her before, but the feeling of being in trouble with a girl with long hair was vaguely familiar. So was his general sense of bewilderment as to the cause of the girl's fury.

'Look, please, just stop... *beating* me, and

let me think for a minute, will you?' He put his hands to his head. The throb of the engine wasn't helping.

'So you're Emily,' he said at last.

'Well, I told you that!'

'And we're on an alien spaceship.'

She blinked. 'Is that where we are?'

'Er, *look*.' Rory gestured around. 'What else is this going to be?'

'How am I supposed to know? You're the one who knew what was going on!'

'You're the one that ran off!'

'Ooh, so you remember that! You rotten liar! What else do you remember, I wonder?'

'Excuse me! Blow to the head! Fatal injury of fatal death!'

They glared furiously at each other for a few moments, and then Emily began to laugh.

'You look so cross it's comical. Sorry, Mr Williams, but you're about as scary as a rabbit!'

'Right. OK. So we've established that I'm Rory, you're Emily, we're on an alien spaceship, and that I'm a figure of fun. We're definitely getting somewhere.' He sighed. 'But what we're doing here is anyone's guess.'

'You said you were looking for the engine,' Emily said unexpectedly. 'You were going to dismantle it. You said the engine was leaking.'

'I said all that? Doesn't sound like me. Sounds... um, well, competent. What else did I say?'

'Not much. You came into the pub, walked me halfway home, and then told me you had to find a machine in Swallow Woods to take it away. That was about the size of it. Oh, you said you weren't a spy, but I'm starting to think you are. One of ours, though. I bet it's some Hun war machine you're after. And I'll tell you something else for nothing – I wish I'd never laid eyes on you!'

'A spy? That doesn't sound much like me either.' Rory stood up and looked round. There were two exits from the room – one on their left, one on their right – dark archways without doors and not much clue as to what might lie beyond them. 'Right. Er. Which way shall we go?'

'Oh, for heaven's sake! Do you have a coin?'

'What? Oh.' Rory rummaged in his pocket and found a ten pence piece. 'Will that do?'

'That'll do fine. Heads, we go left; tails, we go right.'

Emily flicked the coin into the air and it fell on the ground with a clatter. She stooped to pick it up. 'Heads it is... Here, whose head's that? Is this a foreign coin? You're not a bloomin' Hun after all, are you? That'd be the absolute limit…' She turned the coin over. 'Ten pence. Two-thousand-and-nine. You know, Mr Williams,' she said, as she handed the coin back, 'if I thought about it too much, I could be very scared of you. Nothing queer ever happened to me before I met you. Now look where I am. You could be a villain for all I know – following young women, luring them into the woods. I wish I knew if I could trust you.'

She sounded so woeful that Rory couldn't help but feel a stab of sympathy for her. 'I don't feel like a villain,' he said, 'but then I don't suppose anyone does.' He nodded at the left-hand door. 'Do you like the look of that way?'

'Not much,' Emily admitted.

'Me neither. Let's go the other way.' He put the coin in his pocket, and his fingers brushed against something metal. He pulled out a small triangular object on which green lights were flashing. Something tugged hard at the back of his mind, but when he fumbled around for the memory, all he found was a black hole.

He showed the device to Emily. 'Any idea?'

She shook her head ruefully. 'You never showed me that. Here, what d'you think the buttons do?'

Rory's thumb hesitated over one of them. But you couldn't be too careful.

'Best not,' he said, and shoved the triangulator back into his pocket. 'OK. Right-hand door it is.'

*England, now, much closer to closing time*

'But we haven't heard a peep out of Rory since we left him in 1917,' Amy told Jess. 'Look, I know it's a lot to take on board all at once, but I've found that if you don't bother worrying about how it can possibly make sense, it suddenly all makes sense. If I'm making any sense.'

They were sitting in Jess's car, which she had parked on Long Lane, near the start of the footpath that led across the fields past Swallow Woods. A century earlier, Rory and Emily had passed this way, before vanishing.

'Oh, I'm following you,' Jess said. 'I'm not sure I like where it's taking me, but I'm following you. Carry on.'

Amy began winding her scarf back round her neck. 'OK, so we waited and we waited. I was supposed to go after Laura into Swallow Woods, but we didn't get the signal from Rory in time. Next thing we knew, Laura was gone. We hopped back to 1917 to take a look, and there was Rory heading into the woods with Emily.' She frowned. 'Oh, yes, very cosy... Anyway, that meant everything was still going to plan. We nipped back to now, and I got ready to follow Vicky Caine. But still no signal from Rory. So we popped forwards fifty years to see if there was anyone else we could follow, and that's when we found out that the woods and the town weren't there! We were both getting a bit panicky now – well, I was – because we knew then that you were the last one, and that if I didn't go with you, we'd have missed our chance, and that whatever is going to happen will happen... Will have happened... Oh, you know what I mean! Don't think about it too hard. Not to mention that poor Rory was nowhere to be found... A perfectly straightforward clean-up job. What a joke! Nothing's ever straightforward with the Doctor.'

'The Doctor. Yeah, I've seen him around,' said Jess. 'You notice new people here. Particularly new people like *that*. Tall, thin, jumps around as if someone's put a hundred-and-fifty volts through him. Oh, and the bow tie, of course. Very dapper. Makes him look like someone senior in *Mad Men*.'

'Dapper?' said Amy in disgust. 'That bow tie is a disgrace— Hey! You know the Doctor?'

'Small town, and my job is to know what's happening in it. I know when people go missing, and I know when strangers pop up from nowhere and start hanging around Swallow Woods. Particularly when one of them wears a bow tie and jumps up and down a lot. You're both a touch cracked, aren't you?'

'Maybe. But that doesn't mean we're not telling you the truth.'

'Hmm. Well, I've been trying to keep tabs on your friend. Not an easy job, given that those occasions when he left town for a few days now turn out to be minor excursions backwards and forwards through time. Still, I've done my best, even if my poor car's racked up the mileage.' She patted the dashboard. 'Could have been worse, I suppose.'

'Oh, so *that's* why it took so long to find you!' Amy rolled her eyes heavenwards. 'While I was dragging around town looking for you, you were busy driving about looking for the Doctor! Well, that's great. That's typical. Anyway, you'd have struggled to find him today—'

'—because he's helping the police with their enquiries.' Jess turned the key in the ignition and the engine and the lights went off. 'Poor Gordon Galloway. I think he may have drawn the short straw. At least you occasionally make sense.' She smiled at Amy through the darkness. 'Told you it was my business to know everything that happens around here.'

'OK, now I'm officially speechless.'

'Thank goodness for that... Are you ready for our excellent adventure, Amy? I think it's about due to start.'

'Always ready,' said Amy, and grinned.

They left the car, crossed the lane, and climbed over the fence. As they walked across the field, Jess said, 'Don't you get scared, Amy?'

'Scared? Of course. But even when things are scary, they're still amazing.'

'I didn't mean that so much as... Tinkering with time. Don't you worry you'll get something wrong? Break things somehow so that they can't be put right?'

'You can't think that way,' Amy said. 'You'd be paralysed if you did. If I've learned anything from the Doctor, it's that it's always better to act. It's always better to do *something*. OK, and then it's true that you have to accept the consequences. But if you think about it, nobody's guaranteed a happy ending, are they? Not in the great scheme of things. And you never know in advance what ending is best.'

'Not much different from real life, then?'

'Not really, no. Sometimes the heebie-jeebies

are worse.'

The trees were now very close. 'I think I understand where you're coming from,' Jess said, feeling some heebie-jeebies of her own.

'Ready?'

'Ready.'

The two young women clasped hands, and together walked into Swallow Woods.

At once, the light changed. They were no longer walking at night through a wood on the cusp of winter. Here, now – wherever and whenever this was – it was daytime, and it was summer.

'Oh,' Jess whispered.

'OK,' said Amy briskly. 'Don't worry. This'll be one of those warp thingies the Doctor was talking about. It's a perfectly normal side effect of this particular kind of interstellar drive. We'll soon get used to it.'

'Amy, your voice is shaking.'

'Is it? Well, the Doctor said that disorientation was...'

'Perfectly normal?' Jess brushed her hand through the thick green leaves of the nearest tree sending golden trails of pollen drifting down. 'So as soon as time starts progressing in a linear fashion, and the paths start going where I expect them to go – that's when I should start worrying?'

'That's when you should start worrying,' Amy confirmed. They looked at each other and burst out laughing. 'It's amazing, though, isn't it?' Amy said. 'Like stepping through a portal and coming out on another world.' She frowned. 'I assume that's not actually happened.'

'Would it matter if we had?' Jess said. She felt light-headed; she wasn't sure if it was excitement or shock or fear.

'Well, the TARDIS can travel in space too, so the Doctor could still come and find us – provided the police ever release him. But I do prefer having at least a rough idea of what's happening. You know, minor details, like where I am and when I am.'

They walked on. The woods hummed with life – the sudden sweet chirping of birds; the dry rustle of grass and the crisp crack of wood. The light through the leaves was soft and shimmering.

'I like it here,' Jess said. 'It's as if the birds and the animals have been left to get on with things. There's nobody to hunt them, or disturb them, or harm them. This must be what the world was like before people.' She frowned. 'Although, given what you said about time pockets, this could very well be the world before people. Do you have any idea where we're supposed to be going?'

'Further into the woods,' Amy said. 'Whichever way that is. I'm guessing we'll know when we get near to the ship. We can hear it already, I think. That throbbing sound?'

'Yes, of course, I guess I thought that was the motorway. You know how traffic sounds from a distance. But this is different.'

'Less swooshy?' Amy suggested.

'Less swooshy,' Jess agreed. 'Steadier, more constant. OK, let's follow that.'

They went in single file through the trees. The ground became rough, knotted and gnarled with sudden tree roots or unexpected branches, and they made slow progress. After a little while, the trees quietly parted, and Amy and Jess came into an empty glade.

Here, it was winter. The trees were bare and black, and the air damp with thin grey fog and the moist smell of mulching leaves. The women walked together around the perimeter of the clearing. The barren arms of the trees locked together to form great archways. The mist clung to the boles of the trees, curling around them, so that Amy and Jess could only glimpse the start of the bleak narrow pathways that faded into the darkness.

'Do you know what place this reminds me of?' Jess spoke in a respectful whisper. 'The parish church in the village. St Jude's. But a ruin. It's like we're in a ruined church.'

'St Jude?' Amy whispered back. 'That's the patron saint of lost causes. Your town is *creepy*.'

She walked to the centre of the clearing, where a deep pool of water lay. She dipped her fingertips into the dark liquid and tasted it. Brackish and bitterly cold. Something by the pool's edge caught her eye and Amy reached over to pick it up. It was a brooch of some kind, jet black, in the shape of a butterfly, scuffed and scarred, as if it had been here for ever. She showed it to Jess.

'Pretty,' she said. 'I don't recognise it though.'

'Me neither.' Amy pinned the brooch to her jacket. She imagined it as a gift from someone to his beloved. Now it was lost, for good. Suddenly Amy felt very sad. She longed to see Rory again; hold his hand, joke with him, kiss him, know that he was safe. Where could he be? Was he lost for good? Amy shut her eyes and touched the tiny jet object, as if it could somehow link her to Rory, through time. She could almost imagine that he was here, now, standing beside her; she could almost feel his breath upon the back of her neck...

'Who's there?' Jess cried out.

Amy's eyes shot open. Spinning round, she saw a figure dash across the glade towards a gap between the thickly woven trees. Both women moved quickly, too quickly for their prey. They got to the gap first, blocking the escape route. Jess grabbed one arm, Amy the other.

'Oh no you don't!' said Amy, as they turned the figure round to face them. 'Come on, let's take a look at you!'

Jess gasped, recognising her immediately. Amy recognised her too. So would anyone in the country. Her face had been appearing almost non-stop on television and the front pages of the papers for the last four days.

'My watch,' Vicky Caine whispered. 'My watch stopped.'

'A ship,' Rory mused out loud, as he and Emily walked slowly along the dim corridor. 'But is it in flight? Could we be heading somewhere? And why haven't we seen any crew? Where are they?'

'You said the machine was dead, remember?' Emily ran her finger along the wall, from which a gentle yellowish glow was emanating. The light responded to her touch, as it had to Rory's palm in the hold earlier, thickening around her fingertip as she drew it along. 'I feel like I'm still in the woods. In October. But the air's stale. I can tell we're not really outside.'

'A ship like this would have to be tightly sealed if it was going to be able to move about in space,' Rory said.

'I know that,' Emily said. 'Like something in a story by Mr Wells. Me and Sam used to read him to each other.'

'Sam?' Rory looked around, bewildered. 'Who's Sam? Is there someone else here? Why haven't you mentioned him before? Emily, you've got to tell me everything, you don't know what's important!'

'Oh, shut up,' said Emily miserably. 'Sam? Where do you think he is? Sam's dead.'

'Dead?' Desperately, Rory searched through his memories, but he only found empty spaces where this knowledge should have been. Could he forget someone's death? What else had he forgotten? Who else had he forgotten? 'When? What happened?'

'More than a year ago, you fool! In the War. We should have been married by now. But Sammy's dead and I've got myself lost in the woods...' Emily stopped walking. She turned her back to Rory, but he could tell from her shoulders that she was crying. Awkwardly, he placed his hand against her back and, when she didn't shake it off, he put his arm around her with more confidence, sure that this was the right thing to do.

She wept for a little while into his shoulder, not noisily but very quietly, like this was something she had done a lot in private. As Rory held her, he felt the faintest echo of a memory – of someone he loved very much, that he would give eternity to be with – but before he could grab hold, the memory drifted sadly away like leaves in autumn. He hugged Emily even more.

'Shush,' he said. 'I'm sorry. It'll be OK. It'll be OK again, one day.'

Eventually, Emily stopped crying. They hugged each other again for good measure. 'Pals?' said Emily.

'Pals,' said Rory.

Emily dried her face and gave a rueful laugh. 'Bet I look a right old mess,' she said. 'Stupid bloomin' War. Ruins everything, don't it? You can't get a drink after half past nine, and you can't get married to your sweetheart.' She found a hankie in her pocket and blew her nose. 'And there's that wretched humming again. I'll tell you something for nothing, Mr Williams – I know you said you were here to take away the engine because it was dead. But I wonder if you were right about that. Because this place doesn't seem the least bit dead to me. The lights, the noise. It looks to me like it's still in working order. Asleep, maybe, but not dead. Alive.'

*England, now, shortly before one in the morning*

Galloway burst through the door of the interview room as if he were a thunderstorm howling through.

He found his chief suspect standing right up by the window, one cheek pressed against the dark glass, a look of deep concentration on his jumbled-up face. Since their last conversation, the young man had apparently fixed the blind, which was raised up out of the way to allow him to get as close to the window as possible. The clock had not fared so well. It had been dismantled, and now lay in pieces on the table.

'How?' Galloway shouted. 'How did you know?'

The chief suspect flapped his hand. 'Ssh! I'm trying to listen!'

'*Listen*? Now look here, sonny, I've just about had enough of you!'

'Sir!' Porter grabbed Galloway's arm, holding him back.

Galloway got himself back under control. Pressing his hands flat against the table top, he said, in a much quieter voice, 'How did you know that Jess Ashcroft was going to go missing? We've found her car, up by the woods. Do you have an accomplice? Is it the red-headed girl? You've been seen in the company of a red-headed girl, so was Jess. Is she your accomplice? Or is she another victim?'

The young man looked round. He raised one finger, like he was about to issue a ticking-off. 'You,' he said, 'are a very noisy man. Now listen!'

'I'm trying to talk to you!'

'And I'm trying to listen! Shush!'

'But—'

'Lips! Sealed! Now!'

'Sir,' Porter said quietly, 'it can't do any harm.'

The three of them stood and listened, but all Galloway could hear was the steady pitter-patter of rain against the window. He felt like a fool. 'There's nothing,' he said, impatiently. 'Nothing at all.'

'You can't hear it?' The young man frowned and pressed his ear back against the window. 'I